This Book Belongs To

Ellen C. Gallant
from The Islands
Christmas 1992

THE Snow Angel

DEBBY BOONE

Illustrations by Gabriel Ferrer

HARVEST HOUSE PUBLISHERS
Eugene, Oregon 97402-9197

THE SNOW ANGEL

Copyright © 1991 by Resi, Inc.
Published by Harvest House Publishers
Eugene, Oregon 97402

Boone, Debby.
    The snow angel / Debby Boone, Gabriel Ferrer.
    Summary: Rose and her grandfather seem to be the only people
left in their village who know how to dream and experience the beauty of the
world, until a snow angel comes to life and creates a wondrous event.
    ISBN 0-89081-871-1
    [1. Angels—Fiction. 2. Grandfathers—Fiction.] I. Ferrer, Gabriel.
II. Title.
PZ7.B64593Sn   1991
[E]—dc20   91-13638
                                                                            CIP
                                                                            AC

Printed in the United States of America.

Rose was a little girl whose eyes were full of dreams.

Most people see things just as they are.

Rose saw everything blanketed in dreams of what could be.

The world was much more beautiful because of it.

ose and her mother lived in a village where people had little by little forgotten how to dream. It's not that they meant to. It's just that simple problems seemed to get so big that they couldn't see beyond them. Nothing much seemed to matter anymore, and folks were just trying to make it from one day to the next.

As for Rose and her family, Rose's father had died when she was a baby, but Grandfather had come to live with them, and they loved each other very much. Rose enjoyed nothing more than listening to Grandfather talk about the different things that could be. He had given her the gift of dreaming.

One crisp autumn afternoon, Grandfather decided to take Rose and some of her friends for a walk in the woods.

Soon they came to a small clearing. Grandfather knelt down on one knee, and with all the children watching intently, he pulled a tiny seed out of his coat pocket.

"This is a giant fir tree!" he announced.

"That sure doesn't look like a giant fir tree," one of the children exclaimed.

"Oh, but it is," Grandfather replied. "You just can't see it yet."

Then as he began to plant the tiny seed he said, "Dreams are the seeds of change. Nothing grows without a seed . . . and nothing ever changes without a dream."

He brushed off his hands, sat down on a log, and said, "Now this seems like a fine day to plant some dreams. You tell me some of your dreams and then I'll tell you some of my own. By the time we're finished, we'll have planted a whole forest of dreams."

Then he tilted his head back and laughed a good long laugh.

Some parents didn't like the idea of an old man filling their children's minds with false hopes.

"Things aren't going to get any better around here," they would say. One by one the parents of the village told their children they could no longer spend time with Rose or with her grandfather.

One night after Rose had gone to bed, Grandfather and Rose's mother talked together.

"A little girl needs to have friends..." Mother said quietly. "Perhaps you shouldn't spend so much time with Rose and the other children."

Grandfather paused for a moment, and then softly replied, "All right...for Rose's sake."

He tapped out his pipe, and went upstairs to his room.

That very night, silently and quietly, the snow came.

Large white flakes fell to the ground below and continued to fall throughout the night.

When Rose woke up and looked outside her bedroom window, she saw the whole town covered by a blanket of fresh white snow.

She jumped out of bed, pulled on a pair of pants, a sweater, and her snow boots, and ran downstairs.

"School's closed today, Dear. Too much snow."

Rose grabbed a piece of toast off a plate, spun around, and ran back upstairs to her grandfather's room.

"Grandfather! It's snowing! Let's go out for a walk."

"No, thanks," her grandfather replied sadly. "You go ahead. I'm going to stay inside and read."

Rose walked slowly back down the stairs.

"I'm going to visit the fir tree, Mama," Rose said.

"Be back for lunch, Dear," answered her mother.

Rose headed out the back door and into the snow.

When she got to the little tree, only the very top of it was peeking out of the snow. She knelt down and brushed the snow off its tender branches.

"Keep growing little fir tree."

Quietly, then, she leaned over to it and whispered, "You're going to make it through this winter. . . . I know it's kind of lonely when you're all by yourself, but you'll be just fine. You're our special tree."

Suddenly an idea came to her. She lay on her back in the snow, and waved her arms and her legs back and forth. Then she stood up, brushing the snow off her jacket.

"There."

Her body had left a perfect imprint of an angel in the snow.

"Here's a snow angel
to watch over you when I'm not around. . . .
No one should be alone," Rose said,
suddenly feeling very sad.

A tear rolled down her cheek,
dropping silently onto the
figure of the snow angel below.

Rose wiped her eyes.

"You're not alone," a small voice said.

Rose looked up. To her amazement there stood an angel. She wasn't any taller than Rose herself, with blonde hair and a halo that was tilted just a little bit. Everything about her had a soft glow, unlike anything Rose had ever seen.

"Who are you . . . I mean, where did you come from?" Rose asked.

The angel smiled and pointed down.

Rose looked and saw that her impression in the snow had vanished.

"Why, you're my snow angel!"

"Rose, I've come to ask you for your help."

"My help?" asked Rose. "Why me?"

"Because," the angel answered, "you're a dreamer."

"You know," Rose said, "that's what my grandfather calls me. I bet he'd sure like to meet you!"

"Well, then," the angel said, "what are we waiting for? Let's go!"

"She doesn't even leave any footprints," Rose thought as she hurried to keep up.

When they reached
the house, they looked up
at Grandfather's window.

Rose made a snowball,
threw it toward the
windowsill, and waited.

In a few moments
the window opened and
Grandfather's head peered
out.

"Grandfather! I have a surprise. Come outside."
"Well," Grandfather hesitated, "I'm not supposed to . . ."

Just then the snow angel walked into view.

"Oh my! OH MY!
Now that's different! I'll be right down!"

When Grandfather had come outside, the snow angel said, "The people of your town have forgotten how to dream. They have lost their childlike heart."

"I know!" Rose said. "They need to start having fun again."

"Yes!" Grandfather agreed. "Rose, let's see if we can make them laugh!"

They tried this...

And that . . .

But nothing seemed to work.

Grandfather and Rose sat down, feeling tired and a little discouraged.

"What should we do, Snow Angel?" Grandfather asked. "How can we get people to start dreaming again?"

The angel smiled.

"Sometimes people just need something wonderful to happen to them."

Reaching out her arms, she said, "Come on, you two. Hold my hands."

Up they flew, higher and higher
through the clouds.

"Magnificent!" exclaimed Grandfather.

"Oh," said Rose. "If only everyone could see this!"

The angel laughed. "That's why we're here! Come, help me pull these clouds back!"

All three of them grabbed a piece of cloud and pulled, much like you would pull back the top of a bed sheet.

"Now shake!" said the angel.

As the three started to shake the cloud, snow began to fall. Light from the setting sun reflected off the snowflakes like a thousand prisms, each one changing colors as it fell.

The snowflakes turned from a crimson red to a golden amber to an emerald green to a royal blue, which deepened to a rich purple, changing again to a brilliant white.

Down below, children started to come out of the houses. Soon they filled the town square, reaching up to catch the colorful snow.

"It looks like confetti!" exclaimed one child.

"Yes, or stained glass!" shouted another one, jumping up to catch a snowflake.

"Oh," asked Rose. "Could I go down and play too?"

The angel took Rose and Grandfather by the hands and flew them softly down.

Soon Rose was enjoying the wonderful sight with all her friends.

"Look!" said Grandfather. "Here come the adults!"

Sure enough, the townspeople, hearing the sound of children's laughter, began to walk outside to see what in the world was going on.

One by one they looked up at the falling snow, first in disbelief, then in wonder, and finally in giddy joy. In a few moments the square was filled with both children and grown-ups playing together in the snow.

Grandfather turned and hugged the angel. "Thank you . . . thank you for everything."

The Snow Angel laughed.

"It was fun for me, too. And please . . . tell Rose I couldn't have done it without her."

The angel looked around as the snow fell
and the people laughed and cried
and danced and sang.

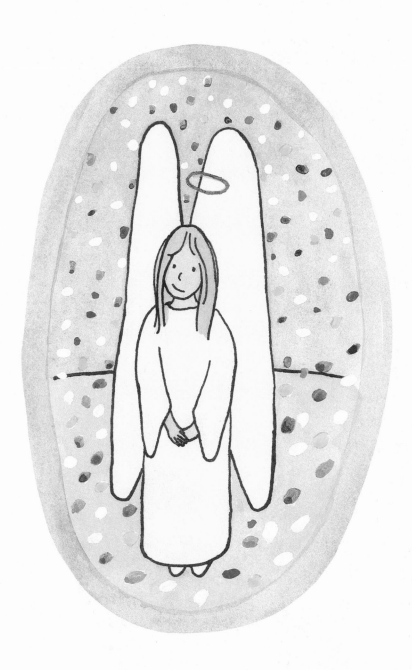

Then, almost to herself, she said,
"Sometimes people just need
something wonderful
to happen to them."

Rose was a little girl whose eyes were full of dreams.

Most people see things just as they are.

Rose saw everything blanketed

in dreams of what could be.

The world was much more beautiful

because of it.